Don't Just Sit There!™

50 Ways to Have a Nickelodeon® Day

Don't Just Sit There!™

50 Ways to Have a Nickelodeon® Day

By Daniella Burr
Illustrated by Steve Henry

Published by Grosset & Dunlap, New York,
in association with Nickelodeon Books™

Kitchen appliances and scissors are not toys and should be used carefully. The activities described in this book that require cooking, painting, or cutting should be performed only under adult supervision or with an adult's permission.

Editorial services by Parachute Press, Inc.

Cover art by David Sheldon
Book design by Michel Design

Library of Congress Catalog Card Number: 90-86411
ISBN: 0-448-40202-5
A B C D E F G H I J

Table of Contents

(of things you won't find in this book!)

But you will find games, tricks, pranks, things to make, party ideas, jokes—50 WAYS TO HAVE A NICKELODEON DAY!

"I'm bored!" "There's nothing to do!" Watch it! Those are the words that usually lead your mother to tell you to clean out the garage; or to take your baby brother for a walk; or to do the dishes. So before the chores are handed out, let Nickelodeon take the word boredom out of your vocabulary!

Don't Just Sit There! is your official Nickelodeon survival guide against the boredom blues. It's the activity book with an attitude coming straight to you from the first kids' network—Nickelodeon! Inside you'll find sneaky stunts to play on unsuspecting someones, gross-out recipes, slimy secrets, and great entertaining ideas for you and your friends.

Plus you can go for the gold with Nickelodeon's Wacky Sports!

SO DON'T JUST SIT THERE!
TURN THE PAGE!

THE END

. . .of having nothing to do.

Chapter 1

What to Do When It's Just You

Flying solo? On your own? No one around? That's fine. Nick has some great ideas to keep *you* busy! So start turning the pages because being just one can be lots of fun!

Mirror Image

Attention all kids! We know you're beautiful! But have you ever wondered about a change of face? *Your* face, to be exact! After all, how would you look with a mustache, bright-red lips, or different-color eyes? Well, wonder no more!

All you'll need are a few magazines, safety scissors, and tape.

Look through the magazines. What would you like to try? A new nose, funky glasses, a big, hairy mustache?

Cut out the features you want. Stand in front of your mirror. Tape the cutouts onto the mirror, directly in place over your reflection. You won't believe your eyes! (Or nose. . .or hair . . .or. . .)

No Soap Sculpture!

Have you ever thought of your hair as a piece of art? You will once you try out this lathering idea.

Creating a work of art can get messy. So first, drape a towel over your shoulders. Now lather up your hair with your favorite shampoo. When your hair is completely soaped up, try sculpting it into different shapes—spikes, curls, a Pee-wee Herman 'do, the Leaning Tower of Pisa. Leave the soap in and let it dry.

Then it's up to you if you want to let anyone see your masterpiece! If the 'do is too, too much, just rinse and try again . . . and again . . . and again . . .

Brace(let) Yourself

Here's a great offer that definitely has strings attached! You can make a friendship bracelet. Start now and surprise your best friend with one! They're easy to make. Here's how:

You Will Need

- 4 pieces of embroidery thread (1 yard each)

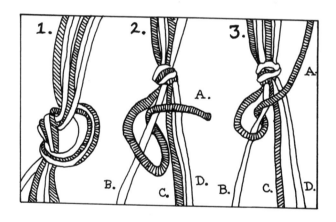

What to Do (follow diagram)

1. Tie the strings together in a knot about two inches from one end. This will be the top.

2. Pick up strand A. Wrap it over and under strand B and make a knot.

3. Tighten the knot by holding strand B and pulling up strand A.

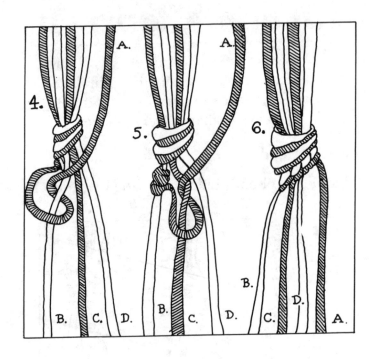

4. Make a second knot with strand A and strand B, the exact same way.

5. Drop strand B. Pick up strand C. Make two knots with strand A over strand C. Repeat on strand D. Strand A is now on the right.

6. You did it! That's one row. Continue onto the next row by making two knots with strand B over strands C, D, and A. With each row, the strand on the left will always be worked over to the right.

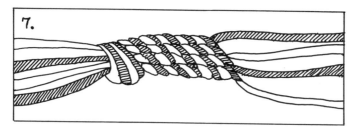

7. Continue until the bracelet will fit over your friend's wrist with a little room left over to slip it on or off.

Deck 'Em

Here's a one-person card game that is:

   a. easy

   b. fun

   c. not messy

   d. great on train, plane, or bus trips

What to Do

1. Shuffle the cards.

2. Turn them over one by one.

3. As you turn the first card say "ace," the second card say "two," the third card "three," and so on, all the way up to "jack," "queen," "king."

The idea is to get through all 52 cards without ever saying the correct name of the card you turn over.

For example, if you say "seven" when you turn over a 7 card, you lose. Then you have to shuffle the cards and start again.

Play it long enough and you'll go *crazy!*

Tattoo You!

You know all about Pete and his brother, Pete. Pete has a tattoo. No one knows where he got it but when he flexes, the tattoo lady does a dance and Pete's mom faints.

Tattoos are just too much for some people— but not for you. You can make your own safe, washable, affordable tattoo in two minutes flat!

Just get a piece of scrap paper and a soft pencil. You can use any color pencil you like as long as the point is soft. Draw a picture on the paper and retrace its lines over and over until they are thick. Now use a sponge to wet the patch of skin where you want to put the tattoo. Make sure it's really wet. Place the picture, drawing-side down, onto your wet skin. Make it stick tight and press down. Now carefully peel the paper off and admire the results. Remember, if you use any words on your tattoo, write them backwards so they'll read correctly.

Tattoo ideas: a snake, a spider, an eye, heart, fish, arrow, etc.

Honey, I Shrunk a Head!

Deep in the dark depths of the jungle, kids know the true secret to playing the ultimate horror trick. Shhh! Come very close. Nick is going to introduce you to the ancient art of head shrinking!

You Will Need
- a medium-sized apple
- a vegetable peeler
- a butter knife
- warm tap water with salt
- beads
- glue
- watercolor paints
- cotton

What to Do

1. Peel the apple with the help of a grown-up.

2. Use the butter knife carefully to carve out areas for the eyes, nose, and mouth. Don't carve too deep.

3. Make a solution by adding a teaspoon of salt to a bowl of warm water and stirring.

4. Soak the apple in the solution for 20 minutes. That way your "skull" won't spoil.

5. Now comes the shrinking part. Place the apple on a plate in a warm, dark place for two weeks.

6. Once your apple is shrunk, glue on the beads to add eyes and teeth.

7. Use the watercolor paints to give your skull a ghastly greenish hue.

8. Glue cotton to the skull for hair.

9. Now add your own touches!

Nick Nose Best

Admit it. You've always wanted to know how to balance a spoon on the end of your nose. You just didn't know how.

Here's how:

Use any metal teaspoon and *your* nose! Heat the bowl of the spoon slightly by rubbing it or placing it in a cup of warm liquid. Then tilt your head back a bit and put the spoon on your nose with the handle hanging down.

What do you do now? Who nose?

It's Slime Time

Just what is Nickelodeon slime? And how can I get some? These are the questions on the lips of kids all over the U.S. But real Nickelodeon slime can't be owned. Like other great natural resources, the mysterious substance comes directly from the center of the earth. Top scientists are still baffled and are unable to explain this bizarre, living, green, gooey mineral!

But here's the good news: you can make your own version of Nickelodeon slime.

First cook up a batch of instant oatmeal, but double the amount of water the directions on the box call for. (Get a grown-up to help you handle the hot water.) Now add plenty of green food coloring. Mix it in so every single bit of the oatmeal turns green. Now let your slime cool (because slime is soooo cooool, you know).

Calling All Boys and Ghouls!

It's a beautiful sunny day. You've got nothing special to do—it's the perfect time to head over to your local cemetery!

Cemeteries are neat places. And a cemetery is the only place to be when you want gravestone rubbings...which you do.

Really.

Gravestone rubbings make great decorations for Halloween or any time!

You Will Need

- thin paper

- dark wax crayons

- masking tape

What to Do

1. First ask permission from one of your parents and from the cemetery office to make the rubbings.

2. Find an old grave with an interesting headstone—one that's really old or has a weird picture on it. You might even be able to find one with *your* name on it.

3. Tape the paper to the headstone so it covers the whole stone and is nice and smooth.

4. Peel the wrapping off the wax crayon. Using the side of the crayon, lightly rub it across the entire paper until you see the design appear. Now just remove the paper and hang it in your room.

Make no bones about it, this project is not for the faint of heart! For more scary stuff, look on the next page!

The Goblin Effect

You don't need a witch's spell to turn your room into a haunted house. Leave it to Nick—and this great special-effects goblin trick—to scare your friends for a long, long time.

To create a creepy atmosphere, read on.

You Will Need

- a flashlight
- a paper bag
- a rubber band
- safety scissors
- Magic Markers

What to Do

Draw a really scary face on the paper bag. With a pair of safety scissors, carefully cut out eyes, a nose, and a mouth. Place the bag over the flashlight and hold it in place with a rubber band. Turn on the flashlight and admire your goblin! Now call a few friends over, bring out the goblin, and turn down the lights. Ready for some creepy stories?

Nick's Pushing Buttons

Everyone knows that recycling is important. So don't throw out that old jacket, baseball cap, or T-shirt. Here's a way to recycle them and at the same time make an outrageous fashion statement! The answer is buttons. Baseball caps and jackets covered with buttons sell for big bucks in fancy stores. But you can get the same effect for next to nothing.

Here's how:

The first step is to collect as many buttons as possible. You can get them from old clothes that are too small or too worn out to wear. Ask your friends and family if they have any clothes they're through with, too. Then check out the family sewing box—there are usually lots of old buttons in there. (Don't forget to ask permission to take the buttons you want!) You'll be surprised at how many you'll find.

Now all you have to do is sew or glue the buttons onto your old clothes. An all over look is great, too. Or you may prefer a pattern like a star or a question mark. You can even spell out your name in buttons. Use all different colors, or stick to one particular color scheme—black and white, all white, or school colors. The choice is yours!

For the Birds

Got a few minutes? Why not do something to help our planet—hey, it's the only one we have. And *you* can help the environment! Why not try making a house out of a recycled milk carton for your fine-feathered friends?

Here's how:

1. Open the top of an empty half-gallon milk carton all the way. Clean it thoroughly.

2. With safety scissors, cut two holes about two inches in diameter and five inches apart from each other on one side of the carton. Put a wire through one hole and out the other. This will hold the carton in place when you hang it.

3. On the side of the carton directly opposite the holes, cut out an arched doorway big enough for a bird to get through. Be careful not to cut into the bottom of the carton.

4. Put some dry grass inside the house. Close up the top of the carton and fasten it with waterproof tape.

5. You can decorate the outside of the house by painting it green and brown with watercolors or markers so that it will match a tree.

6. Now find a tree near where you live. With the help of an adult, put two nails into the tree about a foot apart. Hang the birdhouse by wrapping one end of the wire around one of the nails and the other around the other nail. With a little luck a bird family will soon move in.

7. Don't forget to nail the birdhouse high enough to keep it safe from a hungry cat!

Create a Mess-ter Piece!

Have you ever heard of action painting? It's a style of painting where the artist drips and throws and smears the paint on canvas or paper spread on the floor. The idea is to be totally free. Don't worry about trying to make a picture of a tree or a bird. Just let your feelings, your sense of color, and a little blind luck create the painting. An artist named Jackson Pollock painted this way, and his paintings now sell for thousands of dollars!

Want to try? You first have to get your parent's permission. Then put on some old clothes. Then find a "messproof" place—in a basement or somewhere outside. Put down a big piece of cardboard or several sheets of newspaper taped together. Then get poster paints, ink, or even water-based wall paints. Stand on or near the paper and drip, throw, and sprinkle paint onto the paper. Remember this is called action painting—so don't be afraid to move!

Parent Puzzlers

Let's face it, without your parents where would you be—nowhere, right? But every once in a while, even the most perfect parents have to have the benefit of your great wisdom.

That's why Nickelodeon is proud to present the following public service feature:

PARENT PUZZLERS

Look over the puzzles on the next few pages. They're tough! But the answers are all there just for you. But your folks? Well, they're on their own. First try figuring out these teasers by yourself. . .then check out the answers. Next comes the fun part. Try out the puzzles on your unsuspecting folks. They just may learn a thing or two, thanks to you!

Puzzle #1   Your Number's Up

Within each horizontal row the numbers have something in common and are in a specific order. What is that similarity and order for each row?

1 10 2

5 4 9

8 7 3

Answer

Row 1: the numbers have three letters and are written in alphabetical order.
Row 2: the numbers have four letters and are written in alphabetical order.
Row 3: the numbers have five letters and are written in alphabetical order.

24

Puzzle #2 Choose the Right Path

Can you draw this figure in one continuous line without ever lifting your pen or pencil off the paper or retracing lines?

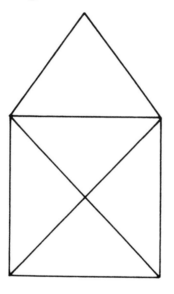

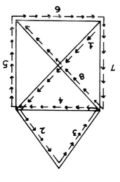

Puzzle #3 The Four Men

This is a famous puzzle first written three thousand years ago. It's guaranteed to make your parents crazy!

Once there were four men: Paul, Jack, Harry, and Bill. Paul seated the other three men, one behind the other, so that Jack saw Harry and Bill, and Harry saw only Bill. Bill, who was in front, saw neither Harry nor Jack.

Paul had five hats, which he showed to the three men. Three of the hats were gray, and two were white. Then Paul put a hat on each man without the man seeing its color and tossed the remaining two hats aside.

"What color is your hat, Jack?" asked Paul. Jack did not know. Harry did not know the color of his hat, either.

Bill, who could not see any hats at all, gave the right answer. "I am wearing a gray hat," he said. How did Bill figure it out?

Answer

There are only three possible combinations: 3 gray hats; 2 white hats and 1 gray hat; or 1 white hat and 2 gray hats. If both Bill and Harry were wearing white hats, Jack would have known he had on a gray hat because there were only two white hats. But he didn't know which hat he had, so he must have seen 1 gray and 1 white. So if Harry saw a white hat on Bill, he would know he had a gray hat—because he knows that Jack didn't see two white hats. But since he couldn't guess, he must have seen a gray hat on Bill's head. And that's how Bill guessed right!

Puzzle #4 Shed Some Light on This, Please...

Three evil criminals were sitting in the kitchen of an abandoned farmhouse on the edge of town. They were planning their worst crime yet— robbing the Third National Bank on Fourth Street.

"I think we should look at those blueprints," Sam Snidely, the gang's fearless leader, snarled.

"Right here boss," Fingers McGill said with a grin, spreading the blueprints across the table.

"Hey Marvin, turn out those lights," Sam shouted. "We're not supposed to be here, remember?"

The third man, Merciless Marvin Strangler, jumped up from his seat and walked 12 feet across the room to the light switch. He turned off the lights and still managed to get back to his seat at the table before the room got dark. How did he pull that one off?

Answer

It was daylight.

28

Puzzle #5 Numbing Numbers

This puzzle will drive your parents crazy—but give them time to think. After all, you have the answer.

Here is just a quickie question: Starting with the number one, how high do you have to count before you reach a number with the letter A in it?

Answer

One thousand.

Puzzle #6 Who's Who?

Mrs. Baker, Mr. Mechanic, and Mr. Cook met one morning. "Don't you think it's strange," said Mrs. Baker, "that one of us is a baker, one is a mechanic, and one is a cook. Yet all of us work at jobs different from our names!"

"That's true," said the mechanic.

Can you figure out each person's job?

Answer

Mrs. Baker can't be the mechanic because the mechanic answered Mrs. Baker's question. And she can't be the baker because her job doesn't match her name. So Mrs. Baker must be the cook. Mr. Mechanic can't be the cook, nor the mechanic, so he has to be the baker. This means the mechanic is Mr. Cook.

29

Instant Ice Cream Sandwich

After all those brain drains you probably need a good snack.

Here's one that takes seconds to prepare, and is soooo delicious you may want seconds.

You Will Need

- ice cream
- graham crackers
- chocolate syrup

What to Do

Take a scoop of your favorite ice cream and squash it between two graham crackers. Dip the sandwich in chocolate syrup and eat! Hey, nobody promised this would be neat—but it's oh so good!

Chapter 2

Two's Company and a Crowd's Even Better!

The gang's all here!
We're a radical crew.
We're def all year.
Now so are you!

Snaking Around

This wacky snake will leave you and your friends absolutely hiss-terical...

You Will Need

- a bunch of kids (at least 4)
- a handkerchief or scarf

What to Do

1. Everyone stands in a line holding on to the waist of the person in front of him or her.

2. The *last* kid in the line has the handkerchief or scarf tucked into his or her back pocket.

3. Now it's up to the first kid in line to twist around and grab the handkerchief. And it's up to the last person to twist away and keep the handkerchief just where it is. Get the picture? The people in the middle get pulled in two directions! Once the handkerchief is captured, the first person goes to the end of the line and everybody moves up one place.

Eye See You

Would you like to turn your best friend into a one-eyed monster? If your friend is already a one-eyed monster, you can skip this one. But the rest of you *watch* closely.

What to Do

Stand face-to-face with your friend—make sure your noses are touching. Now both of you close, then open your eyes. Surprise! It looks like your friend has one big eye right in the middle of his or her forehead! Pretty scary, right?

Twister Time

This is more difficult than you think! Plus, what's more fun than cracking up with a tongue-twister?

Have a friend sit directly in front of you. Now look each other straight in the eyes and say each of the following twisters *AT LEAST 10 TIMES!*

Unique New York

Knapsack Straps

Nice Nurse Nancy Nurses Nightly

Which Witch Wished Wicked Wishes?

When Nick Knocks Only Nuts Ignore!

Betty Butters Benjy's Bread

Freeze Frame Game

Here's a new game the gang can really get into. You don't need fancy shoes. You don't need fancy equipment. As long as you've got a face and a pair of hands—you're in.

Everyone sits in a circle covering their face with their hands—except for one kid who's "it."

That kid makes the weirdest, grossest face possible. Then he or she taps the next person over. That kid looks at the first and tries to make the *exact* same face. Then he or she taps the next person. You keep going around the circle until each kid's face is frozen the same outrageous way. Actually, all the faces won't be exactly the same. This game is like telephone. It's funny to see how the faces change. Then it's the next person's turn to be "it." And so on.

One more Nick Tip: Have someone around with a camera—you never know when you might want a little *Candid Camera* material!

Something Weird

And now for something really weird... This is a quick and easy game that's just perfect for driving your friends crazy. You start out by saying: "There's something weird about my grandmother. She likes rats but hates cats." Then you might say: "There's something weird about my grandmother. She likes beets but hates artichokes." You have to keep giving clues until your friends guess what's weird about your grandma. Of course, your friends can ask questions to try and find out Grandma's secret.

For example, someone might say: "Does she like horses?" You'd answer: "Yes, but she hates cows."

Are you starting to get an idea of what Grandma likes and dislikes? See if you can guess the rule. Here's one more clue. "There's something weird about my grandma. She likes birds, but she hates canaries." Give up? Grandma hates anything that has the letter *c* in it!

You can pick anything to be Grandma's weird secret. She can hate words that start with a particular letter, or she can only like words with a double letter in them. She can like words with more than two syllables, or she can hate words that end in *s*. The secret can be that she hates anything with fur, or with four legs, or anything that grows on trees.

You can make up any rule you like as long as the clues you give are consistent with that rule. Take turns saying "There's something weird about. . ." and change Grandma's secret every time!

Word Golf

Now quit puttering around! Let's see how strong your strokes are! By changing only one letter at a time, you can turn the word "cold" into the word "warm"! Like this:

cold

cord

word

ward

warm

This is called Word Golf. The idea is to change one four-letter word into a totally new four-letter word—by changing only one letter at a time. Each new word you create is called a stroke. Just like in golf. The idea is to do it in as few strokes as possible. You're allowed to rearrange the letters.

You can play Word Golf by yourself or with a friend. If you play with a friend, you challenge him or her to make the new word in a certain number of strokes.

For example: Can you change "love" to "hate" in four strokes? Can you change "live" to "dead" in four strokes? (Answers below.)

Love, Live, Hive, Have, Hate

Live, Dive, Diet, Died, Dead

Nick Trick #1

Step 1. Get hold of some red lipstick.

Step 2. Find a friend—someone who really likes you, so they'll forgive you afterward.

Step 3. Ask your friend: "Would you like your palm read?"

Step 4. Your friend will probably say yes.

Step 5. When your friend holds out his or her hand to be "read," smear red lipstick all over it.

Step 6. Run!

Blow Your Lunch

Hey, dude! Looking for something good to eat? Then you'd better find a cookbook because this goofy game is designed to make you **blow your lunch**!

To play this game get your parent's permission first. Then you and a friend have to make the grossest sandwiches you can think of. But you can use only five ingredients—and they have to be foods you find in your very own kitchen! (BEWARE: Don't make your sandwich too gross. You may wind up eating not just your words but your sandwich, too.)

What to Do

1. Look in your refrigerator and each of you take out five ingredients.

2. You and your friend each take two slices of bread to prepare your sandwich.

3. Now pick one ingredient and make your sandwich. Your friend does the same.

4. Now dare your friend to take a bite out of your sandwich.

5. If your friend manages to do this, you have to take a bite of his or her sandwich too. If your friend can't stomach your sandwich, he loses and has to eat his own sandwich! The same goes for you. If *you* don't try your friend's sandwich, you'll be chomping away at your own creation!

6. If you both take a bite out of the other person's sandwich, you continue. Now add a second ingredient to the sandwich and dare your friend again. And if your friend takes another bite, then you have to take a bite of his sandwich, too! Get the drift?

7. Go on until you have reached five ingredients in your sandwich. Whoever holds out the longest is the winner!

Here are a few ideas for ingredients to make really gakky gross sandwiches!

Tuna, relish, peanut butter, butter, sardines, ketchup, hot dogs, beans, mayonnaise, cornflakes, potato chips, jelly beans, banana slices, chocolate syrup, cottage cheese, yogurt, mustard, marshmallows, olives, pimientos, hard-boiled eggs, saltine crackers, bologna.

Nick Trick #2

Step 1. Tell a pal: "So you think you're so strong! Well, I'll bet you can't even lift your finger! That's right, your finger!"

Step 2. Of course your pal will disagree.

Step 3. Tell your friend to curl up his or her middle finger so it touches the palm.

Step 4. Tell your friend to put that hand up against the wall, palm down with the finger still curled.

Step 5. Now with a charming smile, say: "Lift your pinky finger."

Step 6. That will be easy.

Step 7. Now tell your pal to lift his or her index finger.

Step 8. Now tell your friend to lift his or her ring finger (the one between the pinky and middle fingers). Absolutely no one in the world can lift that finger. Isn't science great?

TOP SECRET!

Caution: These next few pages will self-destruct if handled by:

- three-eyed aliens

- purple-people-eaters (the kind that eat green people are OK)

- Alvin, the kid in the third row who reminded your math teacher that she forgot to give homework for the weekend

- any person who thinks Bon Jovi means "good morning" in Italian

- anybody over the age of 16 who says "Radical, dude" more than once a day

- substitute teachers

- relatives who kiss with wet, slurpy kisses

- anybody who can't keep a secret

The rest of you, turn the page!

Kid's Ink

Invisible ink isn't just something out of a spy movie. You can send absolutely secret messages in invisible ink. All you need is a thin paintbrush or cotton swab and lemon juice.

Dip the swab or brush in the lemon juice and write your message on plain white paper. When the note is dry, pass it on to a friend. Your friend must hold the note up *near* a light bulb (but not right *on* the light bulb). In seconds the lemon juice ink will turn yellow and then brown and be ready to read. So what are you waiting for? Write the secret message and turn the page for more spy tricks!

Look Who's Talking a Foreign Language

ELHORTA OLORTA OUTORTA ERETHORTA!

Say what? That's official Nickelodeon-orta language, the secret language just for Nick kids. It's easy to learn and perfect for keeping your secrets secret!

What to Do

1. Divide any word into syllables.

2. Drop the beginning consonant or consonants from the first syllable. Say it without the consonants.

3. Then place the dropped consonants at the end of the syllable and add "orta."

4. Do the same with the second syllable, and so on.

Let's try the word "secret" as an example. You divide the word into its two syllables ("sec" and "ret") and drop the beginning consonant from each syllable. Then replace the dropped consonant at the end of its syllable and add "orta." "Secret" becomes "ecsorta-etrorta."

If it's one syllable and begins with a consonant you do the same. Take away the first consonant, put it at the end of the syllable, and add "orta." For example, "pig" becomes "igporta."

If the word is only one syllable and begins with a vowel, just add "orta" to it. So the word "it" becomes "itorta."

If the word has two syllables and starts with a vowel, just treat each syllable as a separate word. So "actor" becomes "acorta-ortorta."

Let's try a sentence. "Ouyorta otgorta itorta ightrorta!" That's right, the sentence says, "You got it right!"

Nick Trick #3

Step 1. Lay a book on the floor.

Step 2. Find a friend and ask him or her to jump over it.

Step 3. Your friend will easily jump over the book.

Step 4. Now pick up the book and wave it in the air three times saying "Abracadabra" or any other magical-type phrase.

Step 5. Tell your friend he or she will not be able to jump over the book again.

Step 6. Your friend will laugh and say, "Of course I can!"

Step 7. Now put the book back on the floor—but this time in one corner of the room. No one can jump over it now!

Peekaboo Code

Got a secret? Keep it that way with this custom-made peekaboo decoder.

Copy the peekaboo decoder on the next page onto a piece of cardboard. Then draw it again on another piece of cardboard. With safety scissors, follow the lines and cut out the rectangles carefully. Throw the cardboard squares away. When you put one piece of cardboard on top of the other, the boxes should match up exactly.

Place one decoder over a piece of paper. Write your note in the boxes.

Then remove the decoder and fill in the empty spaces with words, letters, and numbers. It will look like a big mess.

Give the note and the second decoder to your friend. When the decoder is placed on top of the paper, your message is as clear as day.

Rutabaga!

This is really going to sound dumb, but that's OK. It's supposed to.

Rutabaga is the perfect game for when you really have nothing to do. Try it on your next long car trip—or when you're stuck in a dentist's waiting room.

You need at least two people to play, and all the players take turns counting off. The first person says "One," the second says "Two," and so on, until you reach the number seven. Then whoever is supposed to say "Seven" says "Rutabaga" instead. You keep counting and every time you come to a number that has a seven in it or is a multiple of seven, you substitute the word "Rutabaga."

So a game might start like this: 1, 2, 3, 4, 5, 6, Rutabaga, 8, 9, 10, 11, 12, 13, Rutabaga, 15, 16, Rutabaga, 18, 19, 20, Rutabaga. If you miss a "Rutabaga," you get a strike against you—three strikes and you're out. The person left after everyone else has struck out is the winner.

There's a harder variation on Rutabaga you can try. It's called Rutabaga and Fries. It works just like Rutabaga. You substitute the word "Rutabaga" for seven and all multiples of seven—only this time you also say "and fries" for any number with five in it or any multiple of five.

Here's how this version of the game works:
1, 2, 3, 4, and fries, 6, Rutabaga, 8, 9, and fries,
11, 12, 13, Rutabaga, and fries, 16, Rutabaga, 18,
19, and fries, Rutabaga, etc.

This game may not be Super Mario Bros. 12,
but it beats reading those pamphlets on tooth
decay.

We've Got to Hand It to You

Here's a handy game that could keep you and
the gang tied up for hours!

Have everyone get into a big circle. Now ask
each person to use his or her right hand to grab
the right hand of someone else in the circle. No
fair holding the hand of the person next to you.
Next tell everyone to do the same with his or her
left hand. Now that you're all tangled up, the
idea is to climb over and under each other's
hands until you're all in one big circle again.
When you're done, give yourself a big hand!

Nick Trick #4

Step 1. Tell your friend to stand sideways next to a wall.

Step 2. Tell him or her to be sure that the side of one foot, one ear, and one shoulder is touching the wall (see picture).

Step 3. Now comes the fun part (for you, anyway).

Step 4. Tell your friend to lift the outside leg to the side without moving his or her foot, ear, or shoulder away from the wall. You can go ahead and laugh because your friend won't be able to do it. *No one can!*

The Joke's on You!

Get serious! This game is no laughing matter. In fact all that matters is *not* laughing. You have to stay straight-faced, no matter what.

What to Do

Players take turns being the joke teller. The joke teller's job is to make the others laugh.

The joke teller can do anything he or she wants to make the others crack up. There's just one rule: No touching! (Tickling would just be too easy.) The joke teller can tell jokes and make funny faces and dance like crazy—whatever pops to mind! Anyone who laughs is out. The person who holds out the longest is the winner and becomes the next joke teller. And the winner always has the last laugh!

Some Jokes You Can Tell:

You can use these jokes in The Joke's on You! game or whenever you want to giggle.

Where do knights buy armor?
At a hard*wear* store!

What do chickens serve at birthday parties?
Coopcakes!

How do you catch a baby fish?
With a bassinet!

How do tortoises keep warm?
They wear turtleneck sweaters!

Knock, knock.
Who's there?
Norma Lee.
Norma Lee who?
Normally I ring the bell.

What did Snow White say to the photographer?
"Someday my prints will come!"

Doctor: Stick out your tongue.
Patient: Why? I'm not angry with you!

What do you get if you cross a chicken with an elephant?
An egg big enough to feed an army!

Where do cows go on dates?
To the moovies.

What part of a fish weighs the most?
The scales!

Why did the basketball player hold his nose?
Someone was taking a foul shot!

Knock, knock.
Who's there?
Tuba.
Tuba who?
Tuba toothpaste.

Where do sheep get their hair cut?
At a baa-baa shop.

How do you make an elephant float?
Put two scoops of ice cream, some milk, and
soda in a glass. Add one elephant!

Knock, knock.
Who's there?
Winnie.
Winnie who?
Winnie ya gonna think of a better joke?

When do chickens have eight feet?
When there are four of them!

What looks like half a pie?
The other half!

Nick Trick #5

Want to try another Nick Trick? Of course. You'll jump at the chance.

Step 1. Find an innocent-looking friend.

Step 2. Tell him or her: "You see those houses over there? I can take my shoes off and jump right over them."

Step 3. Your innocent pal will say, "Impossible!"

Step 4. Now smile sweetly, take off your shoes, and jump right over them!

Nick-Tac-Toe

Let's face it, tic-tac-toe just isn't the thrill it once was. It almost always ends in a draw unless somebody makes a dumb mistake. That's why Nick is here with Nick-tac-toe—a new and improved tic-tac-toe game. Here's how you play.

First draw a grid with 25 boxes (that's five across and five down). It should look like this:

One person uses X's and the other one O's, and you take turns just like in the old boring game. But the object here is to place as many of your marks as possible in rows. And you keep going until all the boxes are filled. The rows can be across, down, or diagonal. When all the boxes are marked, you count up the points. You get 5 points for every row of five marks. You get 3 points for every row of four marks. A row of three marks is worth 1 point. Whoever has the most points wins. Try it out. It's X-cellent!

Helping Hands!

Keep this stunt handy for when your gang needs a good laugh.

One person stands straight, hands behind their back. A second person kneels behind the first person and slips his or her hands through that person's arms. The kneeling person's arms now look like they belong to the standing person.

As the standing person talks, the kneeling person moves his or her hands. That person can scratch, clap, flap—anything at all. Just keep moving!

Here are some super silly-stunts to try out while in position:

1. Describe a spiral staircase. It's almost impossible to do without hands.

2. Explain how you brush your teeth in the morning.

3. Sing and act out a rocking version of the song "I'm a Little Teapot." Person B can even sing, with Person A mouthing the words.

Chapter 3

A Backwards Sleepover Party

Anyone can have a sleepover party, right? But now *you* can have a sleepover that's a little bit different, a little bit crazy, and a whole lot Nickelodeon. Here's how:

!REVOPEELS SDRAWKCAB A WORHT!

That means "Throw a Backwards Sleepover!"

The Invitations

Let's get right into it. When you write out your invitations, do all the writing in reverse. Your invitations will look something like this:

REVOPEELS SDRAWKCAB   ESUOH
A OT EMOC   YM TA
(Come to a Backwards   (At my
Sleepover)   house)

     Tell your friends to wear their clothes backwards! (Tell everyone to bring pajamas, too.)

Getting Ready

To get everyone in a backwards partying mood, start by asking your parent's permission to turn the room upside down. Yes, upside down!

Turn the pictures and paintings in the room upside down. Hang some posters upside down. Stand your stuffed animals on their heads, and tip over a few light chairs. When your friends see your topsy-turvy room, they'll get in the mood! Then tell them it's time to walk on the ceiling.

Here's how:

Taking turns with your guests, hold a large hand mirror against your chests so that the mirror faces up. Tilt the mirror so that only the ceiling and not your face is reflected in it. Then walk around the room looking only at the mirror. Before long, you'll be stepping over the tops of doorways and around light fixtures!

As the party goes on, try some of these backwards ideas:

- Play Monopoly and try to lose as much money as possible

- Play Pin the Ears on the Donkey!

- Practice mirror writing

- If your VCR has a search/rewind feature, watch part of a movie backwards.

Let's Eat

Usually at a sleepover, a pizza would be on the menu for a late-night snack. But at a backwards sleepover, nighttime is the right time for breakfast! Try these pancake recipes.

Pancake Basic Batter Recipe

You Will Need

- 1 cup of sifted flour
- 2 teaspoons baking powder
- 1/4 teaspoon salt
- 1 cup milk
- 1 egg
- 1 tablespoon vegetable oil
- 3 to 4 tablespoons butter or margarine
- 1 large bowl
- 1 deep spoon or ladle

NOTE: Get your parent's permission to cook. Use oven mitts to handle hot pans and make sure a grown-up is nearby.

What to Do

1. Sift the baking powder, flour, and salt together in a big bowl.

2. Break the egg into the bowl and add the milk.

3. Stir until the batter is smooth.

4. Add the oil and mix.

5. In a large frying pan melt enough margarine or butter to cover the bottom of the pan.

6. Spoon in pancake batter—one heaping tablespoon at a time.

7. Flip over the pancake when bubbles start to appear. Then cook the other side until both sides are browned.

Makes 12 average-size pancakes.

Here are different pancake ideas:

Big Apple Pancakes

You Will Need

- apple slices
- cinnamon
- sugar
- butter
- baking dish
- oven mitts

Take four pancakes and butter each one. Put apple slices between the pancakes and sprinkle them with cinnamon and sugar. Stack them in a baking dish. With the help of a grown-up, turn on the oven. Bake the stack in the oven at 350 degrees for 10 minutes. Use oven mitts and have a grown-up nearby when you take out the baking dish.

Tropical Pancakes

You Will Need

- crushed pineapple
- shredded coconut

Make a stack of four pancakes. Spread crushed pineapple on each pancake and sprinkle shredded coconut over the pineapple.

Rustle Up Some Raisin Pancakes

You Will Need

- cinnamon
- sugar
- raisins
- butter
- a cookie sheet
- oven mitts

Butter four pancakes. Do not stack them. Sprinkle the cinnamon, sugar, and raisins on each pancake. Place the pancakes on the cookie sheet, and with the help of a grown-up, turn on the broiler. Cook in the broiler until the cinnamon and sugar melt. Use oven mitts to remove the cookie sheet, and have a grown-up help you.

Beddy Bye

All right, all right! We know that nobody plans to sleep on this sleepover. But just in case someone conks out, be sure to make it clear that everyone has to sleep in their regular clothes! Those pajamas they brought along are for morning—everyone has to wear pajamas home!

The Morning After

Once everybody wakes up and puts on their pajamas, it's time for pizza! Breakfast pizzas, that is!

You Will Need

- English muffins
- mozzarella cheese
- provolone cheese
- pizza sauce
- ham
- bacon (already cooked)
- a cookie sheet
- oven mitts

What to Do

Give everyone a muffin. Have each person use the ingredients to make the kind of pizza they like best. Then pop the muffin-pizzas onto the cookie sheet and into the oven. Ask a grown-up to turn the oven on for you. Bake at 350 degrees until the sauce and meats are warm and the cheese is melted. Use the oven mitts to remove the cookie sheet, and have an adult help you.

After the pizza, it's time for everyone to say their seybdoog and go home!

We sure do hate seybdoog!

Nick Trick #6

We interrupt this chapter to bring you another smart-alecky Nick Trick! Can you take it?

Step 1. Find a friend to be your next victim.

Step 2. Ask: "Can you stick out your tongue and touch your nose?"

Step 3. After a few tries your poor pal will have to say no.

Step 4. Say: "I can do it!" Then stick out your tongue and use your finger to touch your nose!

Chapter 4

Nickelodeon Wacky Sports

Where can you watch slime-
throwing contests, super-sundae slide races, or
amazing food fights? Only on *Nickelodeon*—or
in your backyard when you organize your own
Nickelodeon Wacky Sports!

The crowd is roaring! The tension is
mounting! Kids from all over your neighborhood
are fighting to get a chance to compete—and
you again are in charge.

Here are hints for running the Nickelodeon Wacky Sports:

1. Always hold Nick Sports outdoors.

2. Ask for your parent's permission to borrow items you need for each event.

3. Try to set up as many events as you can before your friends arrive. That way you won't have to stop the fun in order to do the setups.

4. Tell everyone to wear old clothes and old shoes.

5. Split the group into teams of two.

6. Keep score—the team that wins the most events wins.

Event #1

The Great Toilet-Paper Runoff!

OK, sports fans. This event is really tubular!

The Setup

1. Set up teams of two players each.

2. Give one roll of toilet paper to each team.

3. Give one cardboard tube from a *used-up* paper-towel roll to each team.

4. Don't forget to get your parent's permission to use the toilet paper!

72

The Action

The object of this race is to unroll the toilet
paper and roll it onto the paper-towel tube.
   So:

1. Each team unrolls the toilet paper any way it
   can.

2. As one player unrolls the toilet paper, the
   other player rolls it onto the paper-towel
   tube.

3. The first team to roll one roll of toilet paper
   onto the paper-towel tube wins 20 points.

73

Event #2

The Great Mummy Wrap

What did the baby monster say to the grown-up monster?

"I want my mummy!"

For this race, you can recycle the toilet paper from Event #1.

The Setup

1. Give each team several rolls of toilet paper (did one of your parents say OK?).

2. One teammate will be the mummy, and the other teammate the wrapper.

The Action

1. The wrapper has to cover the mummy in toilet paper from neck to toes—leaving heads unwrapped.

2. The first team to finish wins 20 points.

Event #3

Sit on It!

You'll have to run this event by the seat of your pants...

You Will Need
- pie plates—3 per team
- shaving cream (get your parent's permission)

The Setup

1. Players should be wearing old clothes.

2. Form teams of two. Have each team flip a coin to see who is Player #1 and Player #2.

3. Each team gets three pie tins.

The Action

Before the competition starts, choose someone to be a judge. He or she will decide when a pie is a pie!

1. Player #1 fills each tin with shaving cream until it looks like a pie. Here the judge will say: "It's a pie!"

2. Then Player #2 sits on each pie. (Make sure this player is wearing old clothes.)

3. The first team to make and smash three pies gets 20 points.

Event #4
Don't Crack Up!

For this event you are going to get gakky and messy the Nickelodeon way. Be sure to play **this** game outside!

You Will Need

- 2 raw eggs (get your parent's permission)

The Setup

1. Form teams of two—each team has a raw egg.

2. Players should be wearing old clothes.

The Action

1. The players have to play catch with the raw eggs—*only* with their teammate.

2. Have teammates start out close together, and after each catch they must take one step away from each other.

3. The team that goes the furthest without cracking its egg wins the event and scores 20 points.

Event #5

Buried Treasure

Runners, take your mark! This may seem like a sweet event, but it's easy to get whipped!

You Will Need

- strawberries (stems taken off)
- whipped cream
- 2 large bowls
- Get your parent's permission to use these items

The Setup

1. Form two teams of two players each.

2. Each team gets a big bowl of whipped cream containing three hidden strawberries.

The Action

1. The teams must find the three strawberries.

   BUT

2. Their hands are tied behind their backs, and they have to use their noses and mouths!

3. The first team to search out and eat all three strawberries wins the event and scores 25 points.

Event #6

Dress Up...
Dress Down

Nick wants you to look your best, but not for this event!

You Will Need

- 2 oversized T-shirts
- 2 adult-sized pairs of jeans
- 4 blindfolds

The Setup

1. Two teams of two players each.
2. Player #1 wears the big jeans, and Player #2 wears the big T-shirt. Both players are wearing regular clothes underneath.

The Action

1. Blindfold both players on each team.
2. Now teammates must swap the jeans and T-shirt.
3. The team that pulls off the switch the quickest wins the event and gets 15 points.

80

A-mazing Race!

This event will take extra time so be sure to set up before this wacky race begins.

You Will Need

- a ball of yarn
- a stopwatch
- your parent's permission to use them

The Setup

1. To make a maze for players to follow, wrap the yarn around trees, under bushes, over fences, etc.

2. Set up teams of two—Athlete #1 and Athlete #2.

The Action

1. The athletes will run the maze one at a time.

2. The athletes will follow the maze from start to finish, holding on to the yarn at all times.

3. Be sure to time each player from start to finish.

4. As soon as Athlete #1 has finished, send in Athlete #2. Then it's the other team's turn.

5. Add up each team's time. The team with the best time wins the event and scores 30 points.

END

Event #8
Squash Game

This event is wet and wild!

You Will Need

- balloons
- water

The Setup

Fill up as many balloons as you can with water.

The Action

1. Put the balloons on the grass (not on hard concrete).

2. Then ready, set, squash! The team that breaks the most balloons by sitting on them wins the event and scores 15 points.

   By the way, folks—no hands allowed!

Event #9

How Sweet It Is!

Here's a radical race . . . and a sweet one, too!

You Will Need

- a blindfold for each team
- an empty ice-cream cone for each player
- 2 scoops of ice cream for each player

The Setup

1. Blindfold one player from each team.
2. Place ice cream in front of the blindfolded players, and hand each an empty cone.

The Action

1. The players must use their hands to scoop out a regular-sized scoop of ice cream and place it in the cone.
2. Now the player bites off the bottom of the cone and sucks out the ice cream.
3. The first player to clear out his or her cone wins a total of 15 points.

Event #10

Sundae Stroll!

Top off your Nickelodeon Wacky Sports with a race for dessert.

You Will Need

- 3 different kinds of ice cream
- bowls
- chocolate syrup
- bananas
- whipped cream
- cherries
- blindfolds

The Setup

1. Blindfold one player on each team.
2. Hand each blindfolded player an empty bowl.

The Action

1. The other team member must scream directions at the blindfolded player, telling him or her where the ingredients for the ice cream sundaes are located.

2. The first player to make a sundae using all the ingredients is the winner, and his or her team gets 35 points.

Then the teams eat the treat!

Nick Trick #7

Now for the last but not least sneaky Nick Trick. Have you ever heard of a wet ring? It's enough to leave you "ringing wet"! And your friends will remember your soggy handshake for a long, long time.

You Will Need

- a sponge
- a pipe cleaner
- safety scissors

What to Do

Step 1. Wrap the pipe cleaner around your ring finger. Twist the two ends together to form a ring.

Step 2. Cut a small square from the sponge. Attach the piece of sponge to your ring using the two ends of the pipe cleaner (see art).

Step 3. Put the ring on the ring finger of your right hand. The sponge part is hidden in your palm.

Step 4. Wet the sponge, but don't get it soaking wet.

Step 5. Now find a good friend and say: "You're such a great friend, let me shake your hand!" So much for sweaty palms!

GO AHEAD, YOU CAN SIT DOWN NOW!

The Kids Only Network Brings You Kids Only Books!™

Tune into them all...